STAR WARS™

THE FIGHT IN THE FOREST

WRITTEN BY NATE MILLICI

ART BY PILOT STUDIO

ABDO Spotlight

Disney · LUCASFILM

ABDOBOOKS.COM

Reinforced library bound edition published in 2020 by Spotlight, a division of ABDO, PO Box 398166, Minneapolis, Minnesota 55439. Spotlight produces high-quality reinforced library bound editions for schools and libraries. Published by Marvel Press, an imprint of Disney Book Group.

Printed in the United States of America, North Mankato, Minnesota.
092019
012020

THIS BOOK CONTAINS
RECYCLED MATERIALS

© & TM 2019 Lucasfilm Ltd.

Library of Congress Control Number: 2019942501

Publisher's Cataloging-in-Publication Data

Names: Millici, Nate, author. | Pilot Studio, illustrator.
Title: Star Wars: the fight in the forest / by Nate Millici; illustrated by Pilot Studio.
Other title: the fight in the forest
Description: Minneapolis, Minnesota : Spotlight, 2020. | Series: World of reading level 2
Summary: As the First Order planet is falling apart, Finn and Rey must fight and defeat Kylo Ren.
Identifiers: ISBN 9781532144127 (lib. bdg.)
Subjects: LCSH: Star Wars, episode VII, the force awakens (Motion picture)--Juvenile fiction. | Rey (Fictitious character)--Juvenile fiction. | Space--Juvenile fiction. | Adventure stories--Juvenile fiction. | Readers (Elementary)--Juvenile fiction. | Imaginary wars and battles--Fiction--Juvenile fiction.
Classification: DDC [E]--dc23

Spotlight
A Division of ABDO
abdobooks.com

The Starkiller base rumbled.
The First Order planet
was falling apart!

The First Order was an evil group.
It was trying to take over the galaxy.
But now it was under attack!

The Resistance needed
to stop the First Order.
X-wing pilots bravely flew into battle.

On the ground, Rey and Finn
ran through the snowy forest.
Rey and Finn had teamed up
to help the Resistance.

But the First Order had sent
Kylo Ren to stop Rey and Finn!
Rey and Finn would have
to fight Kylo Ren.

Kylo Ren used the Force.

The Force was an energy field.

The Force could be used for good or evil.

Kylo Ren used the Force for evil.

Kylo Ren used the Force
to knock Rey to the ground.
Now Finn would have to fight
Kylo Ren by himself.

Kylo Ren had a red lightsaber.

Finn had a blue lightsaber.

Finn and Kylo began to fight.
Finn knew how to fight,
but Finn did not have the Force.

Finn was strong.

But Kylo Ren was stronger.

Kylo Ren knocked Finn to the ground!

Finn was hurt.

Kylo Ren used the Force
to take Finn's lightsaber . . .

But the weapon flew toward Rey!

Rey had the Force.
Rey wanted to use the Force for good.

Rey and Kylo Ren began to fight!

Kylo Ren was strong.

But Rey was stronger.

Rey pushed Kylo Ren to the ground!

Meanwhile, the X-wing pilots
struck their final blow.
The planet was about to explode!

Back in the forest, the ground ripped open between Rey and Kylo Ren!

Rey ran to help Finn.

First Order stormtroopers
came to help Kylo Ren.

Rey and Finn were rescued
by their friend Chewbacca.

Rey, Finn, and Chewie flew to safety as the planet exploded!

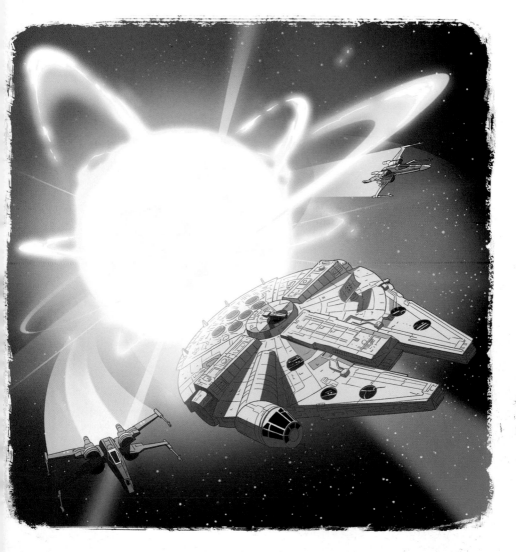

But Kylo Ren had escaped, too.

The fight was over.
The Resistance had stopped
the First Order.
But Rey knew Kylo Ren would return.